For T. A. U.
Love always —J.o.S.

To Mom—for all of our library adventures together,
except that disastrous Make-Your-Own-Halloween-
Costume-Book incident in 1985 —S.V.

————————————

Text © 2008 by J.otto Seibold and Siobhan Vivian.
Illustrations © 2008 by J.otto Seibold.

Book design by Amelia May Anderson.
Typeset in Matrix II Book.
The illustrations in this book were rendered digitally.
Manufactured in China.

Library of Congress Cataloging-in-Publication Data
Seibold, J.otto.
Vunce upon a time / by J.otto Seibold and Siobhan Vivian;
illustrated by J.otto Seibold.
p. cm.
Summary: A fearful young vampire, who prefers candy to blood, bravely ventures
into the human world on Halloween night to satisfy his sweet tooth.
ISBN 978-0-8118-6271-4
[1. Vampires—Fiction. 2. Halloween—Fiction. 3. Candy—Fiction.
4. Fear—Fiction.] I. Vivian, Siobhan. II. Title.
PZ7.S45513Vu 2008
[E]—dc22
2007026620

10 9 8 7 6 5 4 3 2 1

Chronicle Books LLC
680 Second Street, San Francisco, California 94107

www.chroniclekids.com

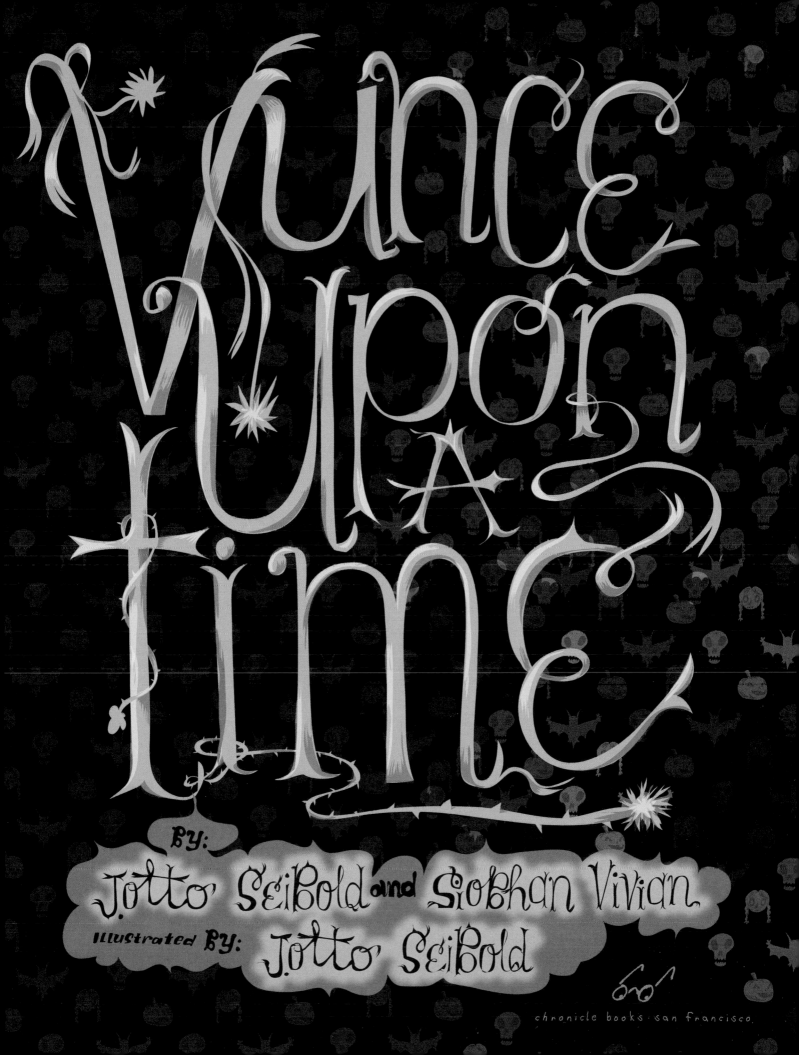

Vunce upon a time, in an old black castle, high on a jaggy, craggy mountain, there lived a young vampire named Dagmar.

Dagmar was a gentle soul. He didn't do many vampirey things. He never flew around or left the castle grounds. There was no need. Because unlike other vampires, Dagmar was a vegetarian!

At night, when the other vampires flew off to hunt, Dagmar tended to his moonlit vegetable patch. Unfortunately, his vegetables grew far slower than his appetite!

But that was not a problem, because Dagmar had something else he loved to eat even more than carrots and squash. Behind a stone in the castle wall, he had a secret stash of  **candy.**

Once a year, Dagmar's ghost and monster friends would bring him a generous gift of treats. But it had been a long time since the last delivery.
And now, when he reached into his stash, Dagmar found nothing but an old, stale gummy worm!
Reluctantly, he ate it.

Dagmar slumped in the corner of his garden. What good was life without candy?

Just then, a little skeleton came by and asked what was wrong.

"I've run out of candy!" Dagmar moaned.

The skeleton shrugged his bony shoulders.

"I know where you can get a whole lot more," he said.

Dagmar had to know!

"There's this holiday tomorrow night," the skeleton said. "It's called Halloween. All the monsters go to town, and the humans hand out candy for free! But you have to wear a scary costume, I think."

Dagmar wasn't sure. He'd never met a
human before. Just the idea gave him the
shivers. But then he thought of all the candy
he could get, and he knew he had to be brave.

So Dagmar leapt into action. He asked his friends for some spooky costume ideas.

"A puppy! He'll chew your bones!" said the werewolf.

"A kitty! She'll tie you up with yarn!" added the mummy.

"Butterflies have creepy wings!" offered a moth.

But none seemed right. None were scary enough!

There was not much time. Dagmar
would have to keep thinking . . .

Dagmar told his parents what he
planned to do. They were worried.
He was such a sensitive little vamp.
So they forbade him to go out
on Halloween.

FOREVER!

Dagmar grew so upset that, for the first time since he was a baby, he turned into a bat and flew away.

RRRRR

"I'm leaving . . . *forever!*" he yelled.

Dagmar soared over the dark, sleepy town.
"I'll never get a costume," he fretted.

But then, inspiration struck!
Inside the general store was
the thing most frightening
to all vampires . . .

garlic!

A garlic costume would prove his courage! Dagmar rushed back to the castle and got to work. A mummy lent him some linen. A spider donated some string. And Dagmar stitched until dawn.

There was only a moment to show his parents before sunrise.

"𝕱𝖊𝖊𝖊𝖊𝖊𝖊𝖑!" his parents screamed.

They were truly afraid! And proud of their scary son. Reluctantly, they allowed Dagmar to go out on Halloween.

"Only vun thing," his mother said. "You must keep that frightening costume out of view!"

EEEEEE

So Dagmar hid his creation in the closet and crawled into his coffin for his day's sleep. When he awoke, it would be Halloween Night!

On the first crow of the vulture, Dagmar jumped
up. He quickly brushed his fangs and then sprinted
to the closet.

But when he opened the door, a blast of giant
zombie moths fluttered out.

They had eaten his masterpiece!

NOOoOoo

Hi

Again, Dagmar exploded
into a bat and flapped away.

"Never to return!" he yelled.

poof!

Dagmar flew over the town. But it was not quiet like the night before. There were creatures everywhere . . . monsters, goblins, even vampires like him! His skeleton friend was wrong. He didn't need a costume after all!

Dagmar quickly changed back into vampire form.
But he was in such a hurry, he bumped right into a ghost!
"Excuse me," it spoke. "I can't see very well."
"It's okay," Dagmar said, "but could you tell me
how to get candy?"
And the ghost did just that!

The two went from house to house saying the magic
words: "TRICK or TREAT!"
Each time, Dagmar followed the lead of his brave
ghostly friend. He hid his face behind his cape and stuck
out his hand, shielding himself from any human glimpse.
And each time, his courage was rewarded with a sweet

The night was long, and by the end, Dagmar's cape was
stuffed full of candy.
It was time to say good night.
"By the way, I REALLY like your costume!" said his friend.

But before Dagmar could explain,
the ghost pulled off its sheet!
It wasn't a ghost at all.
It was a little girl! With pigtails!

A human!

DAGMAR!

Dagmar let out a howl and
ran away as fast as he could.
But the human chased him!
She shouted his name!

Dagmar was about to turn into a bat and fly
home when he heard the human cry,
  "Wait! You're dropping all your candy!"
  Dagmar looked behind him at the girl and he saw
a trail of treats scattered on the sidewalk.
  A human wanted to *help* him?
  "Oh," Dagmar said. "Thank you."
  "Why did you scream and run away?" the girl asked.
  "I thought I saw something scary," Dagmar said.
Then he smiled at his new friend. "But I'm not
afraid anymore."
  The girl smiled back. And together they gathered
the candy and then said good night.

Dagmar rushed back home. He dumped his candy on the floor and counted all the pieces. There was more than enough to last until next Halloween!

Carefully, Dagmar arranged all his treats inside his secret stash.

Then, just before the break of dawn, he brushed his fangs . . .

dove into his coffin . . .

closed his eyes . . .

and started to dream about what could be.